Little Red Rhyme Book

A COLLECTION OF FAVOURITE NURSERY RHYMES

Illustrated by HENRIETTE WILLEBEEK LE MAIR

Gallery Children's Books • London and the Hague

THE BEAUTIFUL AND EVOCATIVE
ILLUSTRATIONS IN THIS BOOK ARE
THE WORK OF THE DUTCH ARTIST
HENRIETTE WILLEBEEK LE MAIR (1889 – 1966).

SHE WAS THE DAUGHTER OF A
WEALTHY MERCHANT WHO HAD AN INTEREST
IN ART AND ENCOURAGED HER TO PAINT AND
DRAW FROM AN EARLY AGE.

PUBLISHERS WERE ATTRACTED BY HER
DELICATE AND DETAILED DRAWINGS AND
HER FEELING FOR DECORATION.
MISS LE MAIR WAS COMMISSIONED TO
ILLUSTRATE SEVERAL CHILDREN'S BOOKS
WITH RHYMES BETWEEN 1911 – 1926.

Contents

Hickory, Dickory, Dock

Hickory, dickory, dock,
    The mouse ran up the clock;
The clock struck one,
    The mouse ran down,
Hickory, dickory, dock.

Dickory, dickory, dare,
    The pig flew up in the air;
The man in brown
    Soon brought him down,
Dickory, dickory, dare.

Lazy Sheep, Pray Tell Me Why?

Lazy sheep, pray tell me why
    In the pleasant field you lie,
Eating grass and daisies white
    From the morning 'til the night?
Ev'rything can something do,
    But what kind of use are you?

"Nay, my little master, nay,
    Do not serve me so, I pray;
Don't you see the wool that grows
    On my back to make your clothes?
Cold, ah, very cold you'd be
    If you had not wool from me."

Little Jack Horner

Little Jack Horner
    Sat in the corner,
Eating a Christmas pie;
    He put in his thumb,
    And pulled out a plumb,
And said, What a good boy am I!

Sing a Song of Sixpence

Sing a song of sixpence,
    A pocket full of rye;
Four and twenty blackbirds,
    Baked in a pie.

When the pie was opened,
    The birds began to sing;
Was not that a dainty dish,
    To set before the king?

The king was in his counting-house,
    Counting out his money;
The queen was in the parlour,
    Eating bread and honey.

The maid was in the garden,
    Hanging out the clothes,
When down came a blackbird,
    And pecked off her nose.

Little Tommy Tucker

Little Tommy Tucker,
    Sings for his supper:
What shall we give him?
    White bread and butter.
How shall he cut it
    Without e'er knife?
How will he be married
    Without e'er wife?

The North Wind Doth Blow

The north wind doth blow,
    And we shall have snow,
And what will poor robin do then,
    Poor thing?
He'll sit in a barn,
    And keep himself warm,
And hide his head under his wing.
    Poor thing!

Little Bo-Peep

Little Bo-peep has lost her sheep,
    And can't tell where to find them;
      Leave them alone
      And they'll come home,
Bringing their tails behind them.

Little Bo-peep fell fast asleep,
And dreamt she heard them bleating;
      But when she awoke,
      She found it a joke,
For they were still a-Fleeting.

Then up she took her little crook,
Determined for to find them;
      She found them indeed,
      But it made her heart bleed,
For they'd left their tails behind them.

It happened one day, as Bo-peep did stray
Into a meadow hard by,
      There she espied
      Their tails side by side,
All hung on a tree to dry.

She heaved a sigh, and wiped her eye,
And over the hillocks went rambling.
      And tried what she could,
      As a shepherdess should,
To tack again each to its lambkin.

Baa, Baa, Black Sheep

Baa, baa, black sheep,
    Have you any wool?
Yes, sir, yes, sir,
    Three bags full;
One for the master,
    And one for the dame,
And one for the little boy
    Who lives down the lane.

Little Miss Muffett

Little Miss Muffet
   Sat on a tuffet,
Eating her curds and whey;
   There came a big spider,
Who sat down beside her
   And frightened Miss Muffet away.

Sleep, Baby, Sleep

Sleep, baby, sleep,
    Our cottage vale is deep;
The little lamb is on the green,
    With woolly fleece so soft and clean—
Sleep, baby, sleep.

Sleep, baby, sleep,
    Thy rest shall angels keep:
While on the grass the lamb shall feed,
    And never suffer want or need.
Sleep, baby, sleep.

Sleep, baby, sleep,
    Down where the woodbines creep;
Be always like the lamb so mild,
    A kind, and sweet, and gentle child.
Sleep, baby, sleep.